My 1-2-3 Bible

Crystal Bowman

Illustrated by
Claudine Gévry

BakerBooks

Grand Rapids, Michigan

God created ONE big sun

And put it way up high.

Every day it gives us light

And shines all through the sky.

Genesis 1

2

TWO of every animal
Went on Noah's boat.
Pitter-patter went the rain,
And soon they were afloat.

Genesis 7

Daniel said THREE prayers to God
Each and every day.
Even when the king said no,
Daniel knelt to pray.

Daniel 6:1–11

4

On the roof were FOUR strong men
Who helped a sickly man.
Jesus said, "Get up and walk!"
And out the door he ran.

Mark 2:1–12

Jesus took FIVE little loaves.
He blessed and broke the bread.
And through a happy miracle
Five thousand mouths were fed.

Matthew 14:14–21

6

God worked hard for SIX long days

To make the land and seas,

The planets and the animals,

The mountains and the trees.

Genesis 1

7

When Naaman took his SEVEN baths
Just like Elisha said,
All his sores were washed away,
From his toes up to his head.

2 Kings 5:1–14

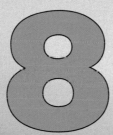

8

Josiah the king was EIGHT years old.
He wanted to do what was right.
And everything Josiah did
Was pleasing in God's sight.

2 Kings 22:1–2

9

God sent the plague of darkness
To cover Egypt's land.
This plague was number NINE
From God's almighty hand.

Exodus 10:21–23

10

Jesus healed TEN lepers,

And they were glad that day.

But only one said thank you.

The rest just walked away.

Luke 17:11–19

Numbers, numbers everywhere!
How many can you say?
Count to 10, then say a prayer
For God to bless your day.

Text © 2004 by Crystal Bowman
Illustrations © 2004 by Claudine Gévry

Published by Baker Books
a division of Baker Publishing Group
P.O. Box 6287, Grand Rapids, MI 49516-6287
www.bakerbooks.com

Printed in the United States of America

Published in association with the literary agency of Ann Spangler and Company, 1420
Pontiac Road Southeast, Grand Rapids, Michigan 49506.

Library of Congress Cataloging-in-Publication Data is on file at the Library of
Congress, Washington, D.C.

ISBN 0-8010-4515-0

The illustrations in this book were rendered in soft pastel.
The text type is set in Utopia.
The display type is set in Helvetica.

Art Direction by Paula Gibson
Design by Brian Brunsting

10

TEN tiny twinkling stars
Are shining clear and bright.
I know that God is watching me
All through the starry night.

He who watches over you won't get tired. Psalm 121:3

7

8

Say your numbers one more time.

Let's start with 1 and 2.

Then thank God for the promises

He gives to me and you.

9

10

Crystal Bowman is a lyricist, poet, and author of thirty books for children, including the Little Blessing Series for children. She's also written a women's devotional, *Meditations for Moms*. As a former preschool director and teacher with a background in early childhood development and education, she still makes many school presentations and loves reading to children. Her two books of humorous poetry, *Cracks in the Sidewalk* and *If Peas Could Taste Like Candy* are favorites in the classroom. Crystal is involved in MOPS (Mothers of Preschoolers) as a writer and speaker. She and her husband live in Michigan and are the parents of three grown children.

Claudine Gévry is a children's book illustrator who lives with her Japanese nightingale named Fuji in Montreal, Canada. Her work is published by Candlewick Press, Harcourt, Scholastic, Time Life Books, Publications International, and *Weekly Reader*, as well as Monotype Composition, MSC International, and Canada's Ciel d'images and Tye Sil Corp. A visual arts graduate from the University of Quebec, and the daughter of a writer, Claudine has always loved books, though she began her career in television—illustrating and art directing an animated film for the National Film Board of Canada.

1

God gave to us ONE Bible
That tells of God's great love
And Jesus Christ, his only Son,
Who came from heaven above.

God loved the world so much
that he gave his one and only Son. John 3:16

2

I fold TWO hands to say a prayer;

God hears me when I pray.

He promises to listen

To all I have to say.

Call out to me. I will answer you. Jeremiah 33:3

3

Every day God gives to me
THREE tasty meals to eat.
Bananas, cheese, and carrots,
And apples juicy sweet.

He gives food to hungry people. Psalm 146:7

4

FOUR bright flowers in a row
Blossom in the spring.
It's God who makes the flowers grow;
He cares for everything.

The earth belongs to the LORD.
And so does everything in it. Psalm 24:1

5

I know FIVE little teardrops
Will only last awhile.
For God will help and comfort me,
And soon I'll wear a smile.

He comforts us in all our troubles.
2 Corinthians 1:4

6

I have SIX friends who play with me;
We run and laugh and slide.
But Jesus also is my friend—
He stays right by my side.

You are my friends if you do what I command. John 15:14

7

I like to count the puffy clouds—
Today I counted SEVEN.
Someday I'll rise above the clouds
And live with God in heaven.

*Then everyone who believes in him
can live with God forever. John 3:15*

8

I see EIGHT little sparrows
Singing in the tree.
God promises to care for them;
I know he'll care for me.

My God will meet all your needs. Philippians 4:19

9

In my family we have NINE,
With grandmas and grandpas too.
We ask the Lord to bless us
In everything we do.

His faithfulness continues through all generations.
Psalm 100:5 NIV